WORKING HARD WITH THE MIGHTY LOADER™

Written by Justine Korman
Illustrated by Steven James Petruccio

SCHOLASTIC INC.
New York   Toronto   London   Auckland   Sydney

ISBN 0-590-47302-6

Copyright © 1993 by Tonka Corporation.
All rights reserved. Published by Scholastic Inc.
by arrangement with Tonka Corporation, 1027 Newport Avenue,
Pawtucket, RI 02862.
MIGHTY TONKA is a trademark of Tonka Corporation.

12 11 10 9 8 7 6   4 5 6 7 8/9

Printed in the U.S.A.   24

First Scholastic printing, November 1993

Steve drives a Mighty Loader.
He is always busy. This week
he has six different jobs.

MONDAY. Steve and his loader are on their way to help build a new store. This job is miles away in the city.

But the Mighty Loader is too slow to ride on the highway.
So a powerful dump truck carries the loader on a trailer.
Steve rides in front with the dump truck driver.

Soon Steve and his loader arrive at the construction site.

Even though it's early morning, the construction site is
already busy.
"Thanks for the lift!" Steve tells the dump truck driver.
Then he carefully backs his loader down from the trailer.

A bulldozer and a backhoe are hard at work preparing the foundation for the new store. Steve's job is to remove the loose dirt piled up around the hole.

He scoops up a heap of dirt with the loader's big bucket. Steve uses the controls inside the cab to move the bucket. He knows just how much dirt to pick up. Taking too little would slow down the work. If he takes too much, the dirt could spill out the back.

Steve lifts the loader's bucket over the side of a
big dump truck. He tilts the bucket to empty the
dirt into the dump truck's bed. The dirt thumps and
the rocks clang as they hit the empty, metal truck bed.

But the dump truck doesn't stay empty long! All through the day, Steve and the Mighty Loader fill up one dump truck after another. Steve and the loader work hard!

TUESDAY. Steve and the Mighty Loader are helping
to make a new road to a school. A grader breaks up
the hard dirt with its metal blade.

A bulldozer levels the ground and pushes the dirt to the side of the road. Back and forth all day, Steve's loader carries the dirt away.

On the way home, the loader moves slowly.
It is a heavy piece of equipment, so it can't go fast.
Steve lets the other drivers pass him on the road.

But nobody is allowed to pass a school bus.
Steve waits behind the bus until everyone gets
off and the red lights stop flashing.

WEDNESDAY. Today Steve is at the zoo.
But he isn't going to visit the animals.

Steve and the Mighty Loader are helping to make
ditches for pipes. They remove the dirt that
the large trencher digs out.

When the ditches are ready, a crane lowers the pipes into place.

These pipes will bring fresh water to the new Penguin Palace.

When his job is done, Steve watches the cement mixer pour concrete. The mixer whirs round and round. Then a chute is lowered and the concrete comes pouring down.

It's the end of the day, and Steve stops at the snack truck for dinner. A special stove in the back of the truck is used to cook hamburgers and hot dogs. A small refrigerator keeps sodas and juice cans cold.

THURSDAY. Steve and the Mighty Loader are working on a farm. The farmer is leveling a new field for planting.

Fields have to be flat. Otherwise, low parts would get too much water and high parts would not get enough.

MILK

The farmer sells the soil he doesn't use to a nursery, a store that grows and sells plants. The nursery has sent a dump truck to pick up the soil.

Steve wants to fill up the truck's bed evenly.
So he empties the loader's bucket into the front of
the dump truck's bed ... then the back ...
then the front again.

FRIDAY. Steve and the Mighty Loader have a very different job today.

They are working at a coal mine.
Other loaders are already hard at work.

A special loader carries coal inside the narrow mine.
A crawler loader uses its heavy treads to roll over
soft sand.

Steve's loader fills a quarry dump truck with rocks.
Miners must dig through lots of rock before
they reach coal. The dump truck carries these rocks
away to be ground into gravel for roads.

SATURDAY. Steve and the Mighty Loader go to their last job. Today Steve is helping to build a new swimming pool in his neighborhood park.

SUNDAY. Steve and his loader have worked hard all week. This is the day Steve washes the loader. Tomorrow Steve and the Mighty Loader will get busy — and *dirty* — all over again!